ONCE,
SAID DARLENE

by William Sleator

pictures by Steven Kellogg

A Fat Cat Book

E. P. DUTTON NEW YORK

Text copyright © 1979 by William Sleator
Illustrations copyright © 1979 by Steven Kellogg

Library of Congress Cataloging in Publication Data

Sleator, William.   Once, said Darlene.
(A Fat cat book)

SUMMARY: Darlene's stories sound unbelievable
but she insists they are all true.
[1. Fantasy] I. Kellogg, Steven. II. Title. III. Series.
PZ7.S6313On 1979 [E] 78-12643 ISBN 0-525-36410-2

Published in the United States by E. P. Dutton, a Division
of Sequoia-Elsevier Publishing Company, Inc., New York

Published simultaneously in Canada by Clarke,
Irwin & Company Limited, Toronto and Vancouver

Editor: Ann Durell   Designer: Riki Levinson
Printed in the U.S.A.   First Edition   10 9 8 7 6 5 4 3 2 1

This book is dedicated to Paul Rhode,
who always tells the truth—I think.
W.S.

For Vanessa
S.K.

Contents

The Jungle

Darlene liked to make up stories.

"Once," said Darlene, "I was

in the jungle."

"We went down the river on
a white boat. On the banks were
big flowers. The trees were so
tall that all the light was green."

"Monkeys and birds lived in
the trees. Snakes came out of
the trees, to grab us off the
boat. I used my white umbrella
to hit the snakes."

"I do not believe you," said
Amy. "You are making it up."

"No, it is a true story," said
Darlene.

"But where is your white
umbrella now?" said Peter.

"I left it on the boat," said

Darlene.

The Desert

"Once," said Darlene, "I was

in the desert."

"We rode on camels across
the sand. At night we sat by the
fire. We ate food with our
hands. We slept in tents."

"Big bugs got inside the
tents. I wore white gloves in
bed to crush them."

15

"I do not believe you," said
Tommy. "You are making it up."

"No, it is a true story," said
Darlene.

"But where are your white
gloves now?" said Peter.

"I lost them in the sand,"

said Darlene.

The Ship

"Once," said Darlene, "we went
across the water on a ship."

"There was a big storm. The
ship went up and down, up and
down. Water came inside the ship."

19

"One day the storm was over.
Pirates came to get us. We
shot guns at them. But one
pirate got on our ship. I hit
him with my white telescope.
He fell in the water."

"I do not believe you," said
Ann. "You are making it up."

"No, it is a true story,"
said Darlene.

"But where is your white
telescope now?" said Peter.

"It fell in the water," said

Darlene.

23

The Castle

"Once," said Darlene, "I
lived in a castle."

"It was in a big park. There
were many fountains in the park.
There were many rooms in the
castle."

"In winter, there was magic.
Magicians came and did the
magic. One magician put wings
on the children. We flew around
the room. It was fun."

"But then the bad magician
came. And the bad magician
made . . ." Then Darlene stopped.

"I do not believe you," said
Bob. "You are making it up."

28

"No, it is a true story,"
said Darlene.

"But what did the bad magician
do?" said Peter.

"I can not tell you that,"
said Darlene sadly.

The Animals

"Once," said Darlene, "I had
many animals."

30

"They lived in the park.
They were not like the animals
here. They were magic animals."

"I played with them every day.
The animals talked to me. And
they took me on rides. They
flew me up, up over the castle."

"But then the bad magician came. And the bad magician made . . ." Then Darlene stopped.

"I do not believe you," said Mark. "You are making it up."

"No, it is a true story," said Darlene.

36

"But what did the bad magician do?" said Peter.

"I can not tell you that," said Darlene, more sadly than before.

The Fireworks

"Once," said Darlene, "I was

a princess."

"In summer, we had parties in
the park. There were big tents
with food in them. There was
music, and there was dancing."

"The magicians made fireworks
at night. The fireworks made many
pictures. There were fountains,
and mountains, and boats, and
castles, and dragons. We stayed up
all night to watch them."

"But then the bad magician came. And the bad magician made . . ." Then Darlene stopped.

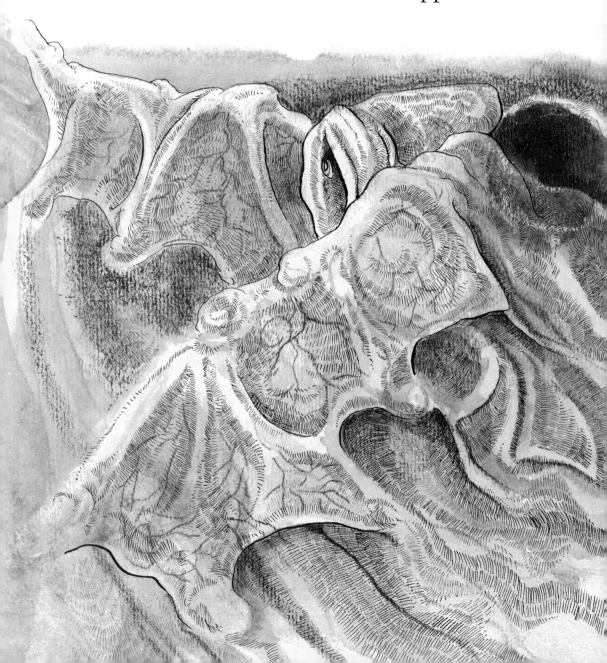

"I do not believe you," said
Sue. "You are making it up."

"No, it is a true story," said
Darlene.

"But what did the bad magician
do?" said Peter.

"I can not tell you that,"

said Darlene, more sadly than ever.

The Princess

"Once," said Darlene, "I was a princess. And—"

"We do not want to hear it," said Amy.

"We do not believe you," said Tommy.

"You are making it up," said Ann.

"We do not like your made-up stories," said Bob.

"We do not want to be friends with you," said Mark.

"But they are true stories!"
said Darlene. "I am not making
them up."

"Yes you are!" Sue said. "If
you tell us you are making them
up, we will be your friends."

"But I can not say that," said
Darlene. She was crying. "I
am not making them up. They
are true stories. You have to
believe me!"

"I believe you," said Peter.

"Then we will not be your
friends," said the other children.

But then Peter could not hear
the other children. He could
not see them. He saw a bright
light. He heard the wind. He
closed his eyes.

Peter opened his eyes. He
saw a fountain. He saw many
animals. He saw Darlene in a
white dress with gold stars.

"What happened?" asked Peter.

"I am home again!" said Darlene.

"But . . ." said Peter.

"It was the bad magician,"
said Darlene. "I made up too
many stories. So the magician
said I had to go away. I had
to go to your world. I had to

tell the truth. And I could
only come back when one person
believed me. And you believed
me! So now I am a princess
again."

"But can I go back?" said Peter.

"When you want to," said
Darlene. "Now, come with me."
And then she took his hand.
And she led him to a white castle
that rose up, up into the sky.